# SUPERSQUAD

## BASEBALL'S SUPERSTARS

## SAVING THE PLANET . . . ONE INNING AT A TIME!

TRIUMPH
BOOKS
601 South LaSalle Street
Chicago, Illinois 60605

ADVENTURE #1
THE SSSNAKEMAN COMETH!
THE SSsnakeman COMETH ROLL CALL
BARRY BONDS
ICHIRO
KAZ SASAKI
DEREK JETER
JASON GIAMBI
JOIN THE SUPER SQUAD AS THEY PREPARE TO MEET THE MIGHT OF THE SSSNAKEMAN WITH SPECIAL GUEST STAR JEREMY GIAMBI
KRAK

ADVENTURE #2
THE MONSTER MASH
THE MONSTER MASH ROLL CALL
SAMMY SOSA
MIKE PIAZZA
GARY SHEFFIELD
ALEX RODRIGUEZ
THE ADVENTURES OF THE SUPER SQUAD CONTINUES AS THEY BATTLE ALIEN LEADER CURMUDGEONLY VEIN AND HIS ROCK MONSTERS.
WOW - LOOK AT THAT BLAST!
TWO TITANIC TALES PITTING THE SPECTACTULAR SUPER SQUAD AGAINST THE SINISTER SNAKEMAN AND CURMUDGEONLY VEIN.
CREDITS
ADVENTURE #1 ART & STORY: STEVE BRYANT & JASON MILLET
COLORS: CHAD FIDLER & CHARLES JENKINS
ADVENTURE #2 ART & COLORS: BRIAN KONG
STORY: RICK LICHT
LETTERS: MICHAEL LOTT
SUPER SQUAD
EDITOR & PUBLISHER: RICK LICHT
PRODUCTION: MICHAEL LOTT

# ADVENTURE #1

SEATTLE. SPRING, 2003.
SAFECO FIELD, HOME OF THE SEATTLE MARINERS . . .
. . . AND HOST TO A MAJOR LEAGUE BASEBALL CHARITY GAME.
SAFECO FIELD
BASEBALL'S HOME-RUN KING AND 5-TIME MVP, BARRY BONDS, ON THE EVE OF THIS CHARITY GAME, STANDS READY AT THE PLATE.
BONDS
25

SAFECO FIELD
ALL STAR GAME
*GREAT* HIT, BARRY!

YEAH, MAYBE YOU'LL HIT ONE OUT OF THE PARK TOMORROW NIGHT, DUDE!

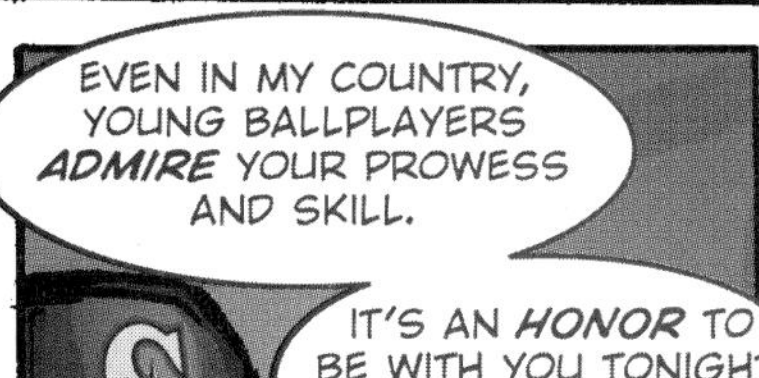
EVEN IN MY COUNTRY, YOUNG BALLPLAYERS *ADMIRE* YOUR PROWESS AND SKILL.

IT'S AN *HONOR* TO BE WITH YOU TONIGHT, PRACTICING FOR THIS CHARITY GAME.

YEAH, BARRY. IT'S A *GREAT* IDEA TO PRACTICE HERE UNDE THE LIGHTS THE NIGHT *BEFORE* THE GAME.

BONDS
25
MARINERS
THANKS, GUYS. I'M SURE THIS CHARITY GAME WILL BE *SPECIAL*.
HUH-?!
WHAT'S *THAT*?!

BARRY BONDS, BE WARNED! THOUGH YOU HAVE DEFEATED ME PREVIOUSLY, I SHALL RETURN!
TOMORROW, I WILL RETURN TO CHALLENGE YOU AND EARTH'S CHAMPIONS!
ALL MEN ACROSS THE GLOBE WILL KNOW MY POWER WHEN I DEFEAT YOU!
ICHIRO 51
SHOOOM 
WHAT THE !?!
ICHIRO 51

WE'VE GOT TROUBLE.
WHO WAS THAT SNAKE GUY, BARRY?

WELL, GUYS, IT'S A LONG STORY, AND I'M NOT SURE YOU'LL BELIEVE IT. IN FACT, I HAVE A HARD TIME BELIEVING IT MYSELF ...
"AFTER MY ROOKIE YEAR BACK IN '86, THE LEAGUE SENT A SQUAD OF PLAYERS TO JAPAN FOR A SLATE OF EXHIBITION GAMES."

"AFTER A DAY GAME, I TOOK A GUIDED TOUR OF SOME LOCAL RUINS ..."
"SEPARATED FROM MY GROUP, I STUMBLED ACROSS WHAT APPEARED TO BE A RITUAL ..."

AAUUMM
AAUUMM
AAUUMM
"STILL INTRIGUED WITH THE HISTORY OF THIS ANCIENT LAND, BUT NOT WANTING TO INTERRUPT THE PROCEEDINGS, I HID AND WATCHED-- FASCINATED."

"I WATCHED IN SILENT AWE AS THE HAIRS ON THE BACK OF MY NECK STOOD ON END ..."

"MY AWE TURNED TO HORROR AT THE SIGHT UNFOLDING BEFORE ME ..."

HEY! WHAT DO YOU THINK YOU'RE DOING?!

SILENCE, INTERLOPER! MY POWER IS BEYOND YOUR UNDERSTANDING!
THE RITUAL MUST BE COMPLETED! OR OUR MASTER WILL BE BANISHED TO THE NETHER REALMS FOR ANOTHER 5995 DAYS!
"HEARING THAT, I KNEW WHAT I HAD TO DO."

"REALIZING THAT I WAS IN WAY OVER MY HEAD, BUT SENSING THAT THE GREEN MONSTER MUST BE UP TO NO GOOD, I KNEW I HAD TO STOP THEM."
STOP HIM! IF THE MASTER'S URN IS STRUCK, IT WILL END THE RITUAL!
GET HIM!
SSSCCHUOOOOK
CRASSH
ONLY ONE SHOT. GOTTA MAKE IT COUNT..!

"WHEN THE FIREWORKS CLEARED, I WAS ALONE. HIS FOLLOWERS HAD VANISHED ... AND TAKEN THE URN."
BEWARE, BARRY BONDS! WHEN I AM FREED FROM MY MYSTICAL IMPRISONMENT, I SHALL RETURN TO DEFEAT YOU!
"FROM THE SHADOWS, A WISE OLD MAN APPEARED AT MY SIDE ..."
YOU WERE LUCKY THIS TIME. HE WILL RETURN ...
EVERY 5995 DAYS HIS SPIRIT CAN BE MADE SOLID THAT HE MAY RISE TO CHALLENGE EARTH'S CHAMPIONS.
AND HE WILL NOT FORGET THAT IT WAS YOU WHO BANISHED HIM.
TAKE THESE FIVE RINGS. THEY WILL PROTECT YOU AND GIVE YOU STRENGTH.
USE THEM TO CREATE A FORCE TO RECKON WITH THAT BEAST.
WITH THAT, THE OLD MAN WAS GONE. VANISHED INTO THE SAME SHADOWS THAT HE CAME OUT OF.
GREAT STORY, BARRY!
MARINERS

"BEOWULF."
I, TOO, HAVE HEARD TELL OF THIS "SSSNAKEMAN." THROUGHOUT HISTORY, HE HAS RISEN UP, ONLY TO BE DEFEATED BY THE WORLD'S GREATEST WARRIORS.
"KING ARTHUR."
"ODYSSEUS."
"D'ARTAGNON."
"HE WAS LAST DISPELLED BY THE SANADA JUYUSHI IN THE LATE 19TH CENTURY."

WELL, GUYS, IT LOOKS LIKE *WE'LL* BE NEEDIN' THESE.

THE RINGS HARNESS THE WEARER'S INNER *STRENGTH*, BUT ONLY IN A TIME OF *CRISIS*.
WHEN THE *SSSNAKEMAN* STRIKES, YOU'LL ALL *KNOW* WHAT TO DO.
WELL, THERE'S NOTHING WE CAN DO NOW BUT *WAIT* AND WE *DO* HAVE A *GAM* TO PLAY TOMORROW. WE PROBABLY OUGHT TO GET SOME REST TONIGHT.

TOMORROW'S GONNA BE A *BIG* DAY.

THE NEXT MORNING AT THE PRESS JUNKET...
TO ANSWER YOUR QUESTION, I NEVER THOUGHT THAT I WAS MAKING A STATEMENT WITH WITH BREAKING THE HOME-RUN RECORD ...
... I WAS JUST DOING MY JOB.
HOW DOES IT FEEL TO WIN THE AMERICAN LEAGUE'S ROOKIE OF THE YEAR AND MVP AWARDS?
THIS YEAR HAS BEEN THE PINNACLE OF MY CAREER... UNTIL THE NEXT SEASON ...
EXCUSE ME... I JUST REMEMBERED I HAVE TO GO..!
MARINERS
TO REPEAT OUR BREAKING NEWS...
A LARGE SNAKEMAN HAS APPEARED IN SEATTLE ...
ICHIRO 51
GIAMBI 25

THE SSSNAKEMAN MATERIALIZED AT THE SPACE NEEDLE ...
... ABOUT FIFTEEN MINUTES AGO ...
... DEMANDING THAT EARTH'S CHAMPIONS ...
... FACE HIM IN COMBAT.

HERE WE GO!

WHILE THE SUPER SQUAD SPRINGS INTO ACTION, JEREMY GIAMBI, YOUNGER BROTHER OF JASON GIAMBI AND A STAR BALL-PLAYER IN HIS OWN RIGHT ...
HEY, JASON! ... JASON ..?
DID YOU REMEMBER TO LEAVE THE TICKETS FOR MOM, DAD AND KRISTEN?
... EXITS THE PLAYERS' CLUBHOUSE LOOKING TO FINALIZE SOME FAMILY BUSINESS ...

HUH! I NEVER NOTICED THIS DOOR HERE BEFORE.

AAUUMM
AAUUMM
AAUUMM

MEANWHILE, THE SUPER SQUAD RUSHES TOWARD THE APEX OF ACTION!

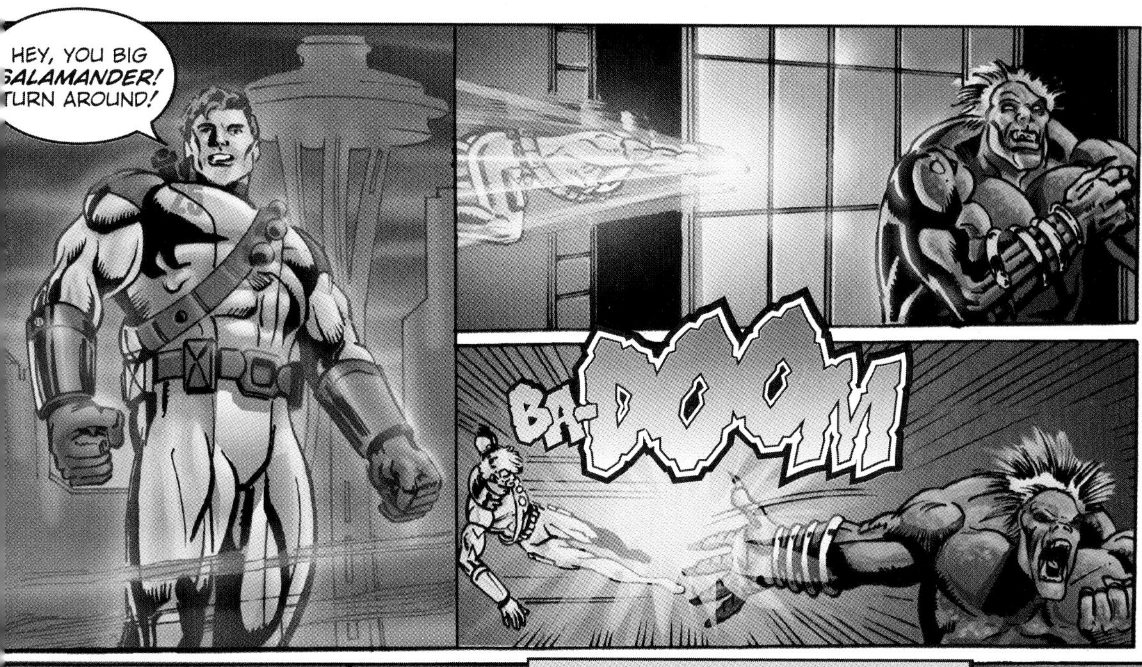
HEY, YOU BIG SALAMANDER! TURN AROUND!
BA-DOOM

I GUESS IT'S MY TURN ..!
SUMMONING ALL HIS MIGHT, ICHIRO LAUNCHES HIMSELF AT THE SINISTER SSSNAKEMAN ..!

FOOLSSS!

SSSHZZZAASSHZZK
TAKE THAT!
FWAP
FWAP
FWAP

OOOMMPPHH!!

YES, THE RINGS GIVE US POWER, BUT WE MUST USE THAT POWEP WISELY! WE SHOULD HAVE REMEMBERED THAT AS THE ESSENCE OF OUR SPORT IS TEAMWORK ...
... THEN TEAMWORK WOULD BE THE ONLY WAY TO DEFEAT THE SSSNAKEMAN!
THE WISDOM OF ICHIRO'S WORDS SINKS IN TO EACH MEMBER OF THE SUPER SQUAD ...

BUCK UP, GUYS! OUR LUCK IS ABOUT TO CHANGE!
I WENT LOOKING FOR YOU AND I CAME ACROSS SOME WEIRD GUYS PERFORMING SOME KIND OF RITUAL. IT LOOKED LIKE THEY WERE UP TO NO GOOD ...
LET'S JUST SAY THAT I STOPPED 'EM.
I EXCUSED MYSELF FROM THE REPORTERS AS SOON AS I SAW WHAT WAS GOING ON AND CAME ACROSS JEREMY HOLDING THIS PIECE OF THE PUZZLE.
THE URN IS WHAT IT TAKES TO STOP SSSNAKEMAN. IT'S OUR ONLY CHANCE.
IF WE UNITE OUR POWERS AND FOCUS OUR ENERGY ON SSSNAKEMAN AT ONCE, PERHAPS WE CAN DIRECT HIS ESSENCE BACK INTO THE URN!
LET'S GO!

AT LASSST! MY POWERSSS HAVE REACHED THEIR ZENITH! SSSOON ALL WILL KNOW THAT THE CHAMPIONSSS OF EARTH HAVE BEEN DEFEATED!
KNOW MY MAGNIFICENT MIGHT! PAY HOMAGE TO MY POWER!
WHA--?!
NONE MAY DEFY ME WITH IMPUNITY! FEEL THE POWER OF THE SSSNAKEMAN!
SSSNAKEMAN, YOU'D MAKE A NICE PAIR OF BOOTS!
SUPER SQUAD, STRIKE NOW!

THE SUPER SQUAD CIRCLES ABOUT THE SSSNAKEMAN, CREATING A NET OF MYSTICAL POWER ...

AAAAARRRGGGYHH!
KNOW THIS, CHAMPIONSSS, I SHALL YET RETURN AND TASSSTE TRIUMPH!

WHEW! THAT WAS A CLOSE ONE.
AND WE STILL HAVE A GAME TO PLAY TONIGHT!

COMPARED TO SSNAKEMAN, THE GAME TONIGHT WILL SEEM LIKE A PICNIC!

WELL, GUYS, YOU'VE PROVED YOUR METTLE IN COMBAT AND APPLIED THE LESSONS OF TEAMWORK ...

BUT OUR WORK ISN'T DONE. WHEN DANGER ARISES, THE SUPER SQUAD WILL BE THERE ...
... TO COMBAT IT, JUST AS MY FATHER, BOBBY BONDS, AND GODFATHER, WILLIE MAYS DID FOR YEARS!

AND TO TRIUMPH, BARRY!

THE TRIUMPHIANT SUPER SQUAD
51
22
25
2
25
UNTIL NEXT TIME. . .

# ADVENTURE #1

# THE SSSNAKEMAN COMETH!

# THE END

# Adventure #2

# The Monster Mash

PROFESSOR KAPLAN & STUDENT PROTEGE BRETT SIT WITH THEIR TELESCOPES HIGH ATOP THE STATUE OF LIBERTY. THEY ARE TRACKING A NEW COMET IN THE NIGHT SKY.
THE MOON LOOKS AWFULLY BLUE TONIGHT.
THERE. YOU SEE? IT HAPPENED AGAIN. I TOLD YOU SO! THAT'S TWENTY-ONE WHOLE DEGREES! SIX TIMES IN THE LAST TWELVE HOURS. THE MOON IS MOVING. THAT'S CRAZY!
LOOK, PART OF IT BROKE OFF.
I DON'T BELIEVE THIS! IT'S PICKING UP SPEED NOW. ITS CURRENT PATH PUTS IT ON A COLLISION COURSE WITH EARTH!!!
THE ASTEROID...
MY READING SHOWS IMPACT IN THE BRONX IN SEVEN MINUTES! LET'S GO!!!
YANKEE STADIUM
GATE 4
NTRY

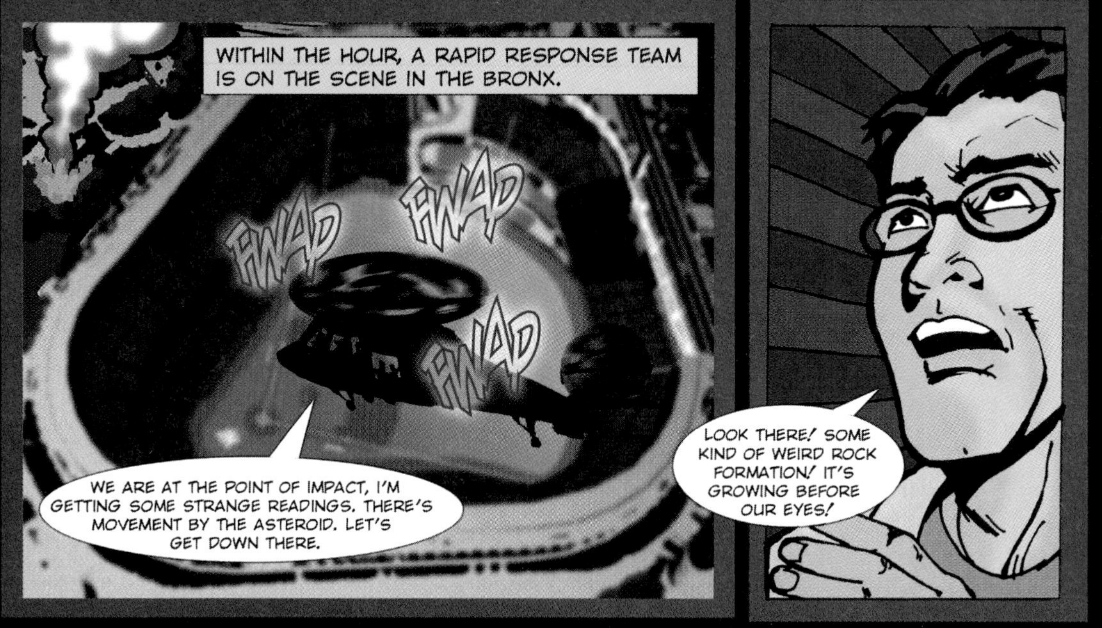
WITHIN THE HOUR, A RAPID RESPONSE TEAM IS ON THE SCENE IN THE BRONX.
FWAP
FWAP
FWAP
WE ARE AT THE POINT OF IMPACT, I'M GETTING SOME STRANGE READINGS. THERE'S MOVEMENT BY THE ASTEROID. LET'S GET DOWN THERE.
LOOK THERE! SOME KIND OF WEIRD ROCK FORMATION! IT'S GROWING BEFORE OUR EYES!

I DON'T BELIEVE IT! IT'S BECOMING A ROCK MONSTER!
KRAK
KRAK

ASTOUNDING!

FASCINATING! WHERE ON EARTH - ?
NOWHERE ON EARTH, I ASSURE YOU.
WHO SAID THAT!?!

OH BOY!
I THINK THIS IS THE PART WHERE I ASK TO BE "TAKEN TO YOUR LEADER."

MAJOR LEAGUE BASEBALL STARS SAMMY SOSA, ALEX RODRIGUEZ, GARY SHEFFIELD, & MIKE PIAZZA PLAY A LITTLE SANDLOT BASEBALL WITH THE LOCAL KIDS.
GOOD PITCH, FOR A CATCHER.
KRAK
KRAK
KRAK
I GOT IT SAMMY!!!
WAY TO GO A-ROD!
GOOD HUSTLE!
THANKS, SHEFF.

A HELICOPTER?!?
WHERE'S THE BLIMP?
PWAP PWAP
WHAT THE
HEY !?!
PWAP

EXCUSE US KIDS, I HATE TO INTERUPT YOUR GAME BUT I NEED THE PLAYERS.
THIS IS GENERAL SUGARMAN, STRAIGHT FROM WASHINGTON D.C. GIVE HIM YOUR FULL SUPPORT AND ATTENTION.
THANK YOU PROFESSOR. I'LL BE BLUNT - WE HAVE AN EMERGENCY. THE WHOLE UNIVERSE IS IN DANGER.
WHAT CAN WE DO?

AN ASTEROID FELL TO THE EARTH EARLY THIS MORNING. IT WAS NO ORDINARY ASTEROID. IT WAS A GRANITE SEED! A SEED THAT GREW INTO A GIANT ROCK THAT WILL ALTER OUR PLANET'S ATMOSPHERE. OUR BEST MINDS TELL ME THAT IF LEFT ALONE, THIS ONE ROCK WILL MAKE THE EARTH UNINHABITABLE FOR HUMANS!
ONE ROCK CAN RUIN US. EARLIER TODAY, THE HUBBLE TELESCOPE SENT US A PHOTOGRAPH OF 73 MORE OF THESE GRANITE SEEDS, RAPIDLY APPROACHING THE EARTH AS WE SPEAK.

RANGERS
3
Braves
Mets
31
THE PROFESSOR AND HIS ASSISTANT HAVE BEEN MONITORING THE SITUATION FROM THE BEGINNING.

THE FINEST ASTRONOMERS IN THE WORLD ARE UNABLE TO CALCULATE THE ASTEROID'S EXACT APPROACH TRAJECTORIES. SINCE BRETT HERE WORKED SO HARD IN SCHOOL, HE DEVELOPED A FORMULA TO HELP US PINPOINT THE DIRECTION, AND IT'S RIGHT HERE IN THE BRONX.
WHAT'S OUR MISSION PROFESSOR?
GOOD TO SEE YOU!
RANGERS
Mets

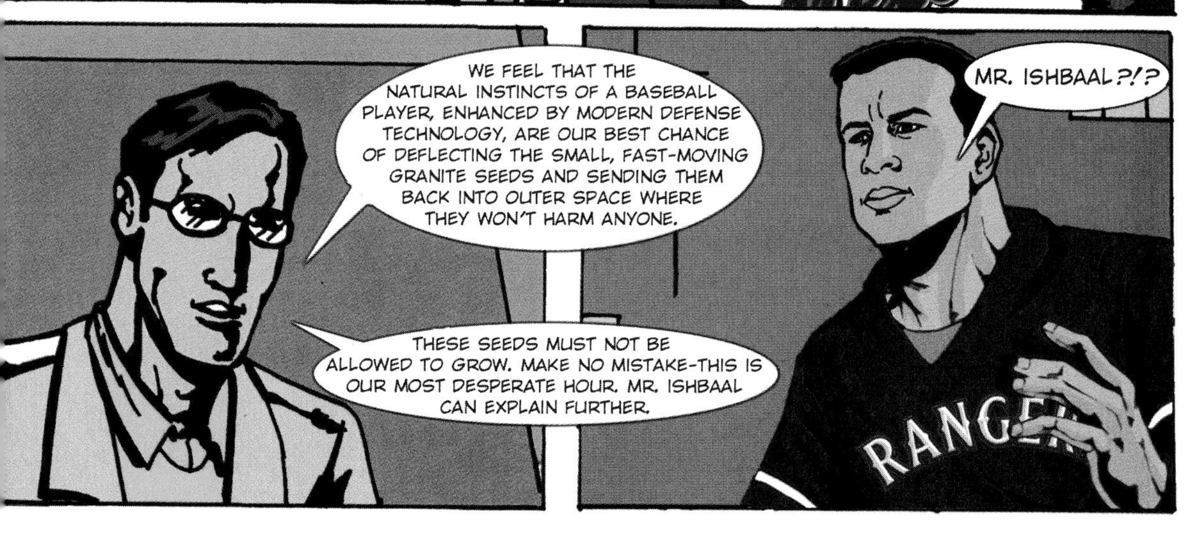
WE FEEL THAT THE NATURAL INSTINCTS OF A BASEBALL PLAYER, ENHANCED BY MODERN DEFENSE TECHNOLOGY, ARE OUR BEST CHANCE OF DEFLECTING THE SMALL, FAST-MOVING GRANITE SEEDS AND SENDING THEM BACK INTO OUTER SPACE WHERE THEY WON'T HARM ANYONE.
MR. ISHBAAL?!?
THESE SEEDS MUST NOT BE ALLOWED TO GROW. MAKE NO MISTAKE-THIS IS OUR MOST DESPERATE HOUR. MR. ISHBAAL CAN EXPLAIN FURTHER.

WITH ALL DUE RESPECT PROFESSOR, GRANITE SEEDS, GIANT ROCKS, FOUR BASEBALL PLAYERS SAVING THE UNIVERSE? DOESN'T THAT SOUND JUST A LITTLE PREPOSTEROUS?
WHAT'S NEXT? LITTLE GREEN MEN FROM OUTER SPACE?
UH, *A-ROD*...?
?
GREETINGS. MY NAME IS ISHBAAL. I WAS SENT HERE BY MY PLANET IN ADVANCE OF AN INVASION FORCE TO GATHER INTELLIGENCE ABOUT THE EARTH AND IT'S INHABITANTS. IN THE SHORT TIME THAT I HAVE LIVED AMONG THE HUMANS, I HAVE DEVELOPED AN APPRECIATION FOR EARTHLINGS AND THEIR CULTURE. I COULD NOT, AS YOU SAY "LIVE WITH MYSELF" IF I WERE EVEN IN SOME SMALL PART, RESPONSIBLE FOR THE ELIMINATION OF CHEESEBURGERS, THE MACARENA, AND, OF COURSE, YOUR NATIONAL PASTIME, BASEBALL.
I HOPE TO MAKE EARTH MY NEW HOME. SO DO A LOT OF MY PEOPLE. ONLY I WOULD WISH TO LIVE HERE AS IT IS NOW, NOT AS MY PEOPLE WOULD REMAKE IT.
OH, BOY*!!!*

THANK YOU MR. ISHBAAL.
THESE SUITS ARE DESIGNED TO BOOST YOUR STRENGTH, SPEED AND ENDURANCE.
YOU ARE NOW THE ULTIMATE SPORTS FORCE!
LET'S TRY ON OUR NEW UNIFORMS.
SHEFFIELD 11
PIAZZA 31
RODRIGUEZ 3
SOSA 21
IT'S AS LIGHT AS A FEATHER!
YOUR PRIMARY WEAPON - A SUPER-CHARGED POWER BAT.
HEY A-ROD, YOU KNOW AN ALUMINUM BAT IS AGAINST THE RULES!
WHOA!!!
HEY SOMEBODY CORKED MY BAT-WITH MISSILES!
31
21

THESE UNIFORMS ARE AWESOME!!!
GEEZ...THOSE ARE SOME BIG PEACEMAKER BATS!
31
BRING ON THOSE ALIENS.

WE'LL BE THE GREATEST TEAM OF ALL TIME.
WALK SOFTLY AND CARRY A BIG STICK!
11

MEANWHILE . . . IN A SPACESHIP JUST OUTSIDE THE EARTH'S ATMOSPHERE . . .
...THIS TIME I WILL SUCCEED. I WILL SUCCEED!
WE MUST DIVIDE AND CONQUER THESE "HEROES."
AS YOU COMMAND.
THEN I, CURMUDGEONLY VEIN, WILL RULE THE UNIVERSE!

OKAY, LET'S GO OVER OUR STRATEGY ONE MORE TIME...

GENERAL, OUR AGENTS IN THE FIELD ARE REPORTING FROM THE LOCATION OF THE GIANT ROCK. I DON'T KNOW HOW ELSE TO PUT THIS SIR, BUT THE ROCK HAS GROWN LEGS AND IS WALKING TOWARD THE CITY! WE SHOULD HAVE THE LIVE FEED ON SCREEN MOMENTARILY!

ALL THOSE PEOPLE . . . WE HAVE NO CHOICE BUT TO ABORT THE MISSION AND STOP THAT ROCK MONSTER. THOSE PEOPLE ARE IN MORE IMMEDIATE DANGER.

THAT WON'T BE NECESSARY GENERAL. IF THESE BATS CAN DO EVERYTHING YOU SAY THEY CAN, SHEFF AND I CAN HANDLE THAT OVERGROWN PEBBLE BY OURSELVES!!!
WHILE WE'RE BUSY KNOCKING THAT ROCK DOWN TO SIZE, A-ROD AND SAMMY CAN CONCENTRATE ON HITTING THE METEORS OUT OF THE "PARK"!
SORT OF LIKE A HOME RUN DERBY!

A COUPLE WALKS DOWN 5TH AVENUE NEAR CENTRAL PARK IN MANHATTAN.
YOU LOOK BEAUTIFUL SWEETIE.

THOSE ARE SOME ROCKS.
LOOK AT THOSE RINGS, OH MY!

DO YOU THINK WE'LL EVER GET MARRIED?
ARRGH!!!
I JUST THOUGHT I'D ASK - WE'VE BEEN DATING FOR ALMOST A YEAR.

ARRRGGH!
NOW THAT'S UNCALLED FOR!!!

KRAK
KRAK
HMM, IT LOOKED SMALLER ON THE VIEWING SCREEN!
WE'VE GOT OUR WORK CUT OUT FOR US SHEFF.
AAAH! RUN FOR YOUR LIVES!!!
LOOK OUT!

CRASH
CRASH
AW, NO! MY CAR! I JUST GOT IT WASHED.

WE'VE GOT TO DRAW HIS ATTENTION AWAY FROM THE PEOPLE AND TOWARDS US!
THAT'S IT? THAT'S YOUR BIG PLAN?!!

SHEFF, LOOK OUT!
ARRRGGH!
VRROOOOMM
WELL, WE GOT HIS ATTENTION.

MIKE, GARY, TRY TO FOCUS YOUR ATTACK INTO ONE CONCENTRATED BLOW!
YOU HEARD ISHBAAL.
LET'S DO IT!
READY!
WELL, HERE GOES NOTHING!
WE DID IT!!!
YEAH! I NEVER THOUGHT I'D SAY THIS - BUT I'D RATHER FACE RANDY JOHNSON!
YIKES!

AT THE SAME MOMENT, ON THE OUTSKIRTS OF TOWN...
LIVE ON TODAY'S SPORTS REPORT WE ARE AT THE CRATER WHERE EARLIER TODAY, A SHOOTING STAR LANDED. MY GUESTS ARE ALL-STARS SAMMY SOSA AND ALEX RODRIGUEZ.
NOW GUYS IT'S BEEN A WHILE SINCE I PLAYED, BUT THOSE BATS CAN'T BE LEGAL!
CAN WE DO THIS INTERVIEW LATER?
WE'RE A LITTLE BUSY RIGHT NOW.

HERE COME THE FIRST TWO! I'LL TAKE THE ONE ON THE LEFT!
I'M RIGHT BEHIND YOU, SAMMY!

KRAK
KRAK
GOT IT!

"COMMERCIAL! LET'S GO TO COMMERCIAL."
TSK! PEDRO THROWS HARDER THAN THAT!

ONE AFTER THE OTHER, THE GRANITE SEEDS FALL OUT OF THE SKY, AND ONE AFTER THE OTHER SOSA AND A-ROD SEND THEM SCREAMING BACK TO OUTER-SPACE WHERE THEY CAME FROM.
KNOWING HOW MUCH IS AT STAKE, OUR HEROES ARE GIVING EVERYTHING THEY HAVE.
3 T
21
WATCH OUT, SAMMY! HERE COME THREE MORE!

ONE . . .
BLAM BLAM BLAM

TWO . . .
BLAM BLAM BLAM

HAT TRICK!
BLAM BLAM BLAM

I'M JUST GETTING WARMED UP!
WELL, WAS THERE EVER REALLY ANY DOUBT THEY COULD DO IT? BACK IN A MOMENT WITH TONIGHT'S STARTING LINEUPS.

AMAZING! THEY GOT ALL OF THEM!
NOT QUITE, SIR. ONE LAST SEED APPROACHING...
ONLY ONE LEFT!
I'VE GOT IT, SAMMY.
IT'S ALL YOU A-ROD!
A-ROD!!!

GOT YOU, PARTNER!
PHEW! THANKS SAMMY, BUT THAT LAST ROCK - !

NOOOoo!

WE'LL BOTH GET THIS LAST ONE TOGETHER. ARE YOU READY?
READY.
POWER UP!
LET'S DO SOME DAMAGE!!!
BLAM
BLAM
BLAM

HOW'D YOU FELLAS MAKE OUT?
THE ROCKS ARE ON THEIR WAY BACK TO THIS SPOT. THERE MUST BE SOMETHING ABOUT THE AREA HERE. WE CAN'T LET THEM GROW INTO ANOTHER ROCK MONSTER. THIS IS IT GUYS!!!
I DON'T KNOW. FIRST THERE WAS THIS BIG ROCK, THEN LOTS OF LITTLE ROCKS. A CRAZY ROCK QUARRY.
BATTER UP!
COME BACK HERE, YOU OVERGROWN PET ROCK!
ARRRGGH!

OUR HEROES APPEAR OUTNUMBERED AS THEY BATTLE WITH THE ROCK CREATURES.
LIKE SKIPPIN' STONES.
THIS IS BETTER THAN BATTING PRACTICE!
KEEP AT 'EM, GUYS!

BEFORE TOO LONG, ONLY ONE ROCK CREATURE IS LEFT STANDING.
UH-OH!
OUR HEROES ARE VICTORIOUS. THE UNIVERSE IS SAVED!!!
LET'S GO BACK TO THE STUDIO FOR A CHECK ON THE WEATHER.

UNBELIEVABLE! ALL OF MY GRANITE SEEDS HAVE BEEN DEFLECTED! ALL OF MY ROCK MONSTERS HAVE BEEN DEFEATED! PREPARE TO LEAVE THE EARTH'S ORBIT!
BUT SIR, WHAT ABOUT ISHBAAL?
I HAVE UNDERESTIMATED THE ULTIMATE SPORTS FORCE BASEBALL HEROES.
NOW I HAVE BEEN FOILED IN MY ATTEMPT TO CONQUER THE UNIVERSE!!! NEXT TIME...I WILL DEFEAT THEM.
I SHALL RETURN! AND WHEN I DO, IT SHALL BE AS THE SUPREME RULER OF THE GALAXY!

YANKEE STADIUM - ISHBAAL TAKES BATTING PRACTICE WITH HIS NEW FRIENDS.
HERE COMES THE CURVE...
C'MON, ISHBAAL! NICE AND EASY!

NICE AND EASY? I THOUGHT MY SWING SHOULD BE AGGRESSIVE AND HARD?

IS IT ME, OR DOES HIS BAT LOOK FAMILIAR?
IT SHOULD, I MADE IT FOR HIM OUT OF THE GRANITE.
LOOK AT HIM UP THERE, HE'S A NATURAL! HE'LL FIT IN JUST FINE ON THIS PLANET!
I DON'T KNOW IF A ROCK BAT IS LEGAL, BUT IT'S A GOOD IDEA.

"NICE AND EASY?"

# ADVENTURE #2

# THE MONSTER MASH

THE END

31
21
11